TALES FROM

№ 4

MAPLE RIDGE

THE GHOST OF JUNIPER CREEK

By Grace Gilmore
Illustrated by Petra Brown

LITTLE SIMON

NEW YORK   LONDON   TORONTO   SYDNEY   NEW DELHI

LITTLE SIMON

An imprint of Simon & Schuster Children's Publishing Division
1230 Avenue of the Americas, New York, New York 10020
This Little Simon edition August 2015
Copyright © 2015 by Simon & Schuster, Inc.
All rights reserved, including the right of reproduction in whole or in part in any form.
LITTLE SIMON is a registered trademark of Simon & Schuster, Inc., and associated colophon is a trademark of Simon & Schuster, Inc.
For information about special discounts for bulk purchases, please contact Simon & Schuster Special Sales at 1-866-506-1949 or business@simonandschuster.com.
The Simon & Schuster Speakers Bureau can bring authors to your live event. For more information or to book an event, contact the Simon & Schuster Speakers Bureau at 1-866-248-3049 or visit our website at www.simonspeakers.com.
Designed by Chani Yammer
The illustration of this book were rendered in pen and ink.
The text of this book was set in Caecilia.
Manufactured in the United States of America 0715 FFG
10 9 8 7 6 5 4 3 2 1
Library of Congress Cataloging-in-Publication Data
Gilmore, Grace.
The ghost of Juniper Creek / by Grace Gilmore ; illustrated by Petra Brown. —
First Little Simon paperback edition.
pages cm. — (Tales from Maple Ridge ; [4])
Summary: Logan and his friend, Anthony, spy something white high in the trees near the water, and after a neighbor confirms what Logan's older brother, Drew, told them about the Ghost of Juniper Creek, they summon all of their courage to set a trap
ISBN 978-1-4814-3009-8 (pbk : alk. paper) — ISBN 978-1-4814-3010-4 (hc : alk. paper) —
ISBN 978-1-4814-3011-1 (eBook) [1. Ghosts—Fiction. 2. Family life—Fiction. 3. Farm life—Fiction.] I. Brown, Petra, illustrator.
II. Title.
PZ7.G4372Gho 2015
[Fic]—dc23
2014036050

CONTENTS

CHAPTER 1: **A FLASH OF WHITE** 1

CHAPTER 2: **BOO!** 15

CHAPTER 3: **THE GHOST TRAP** 27

CHAPTER 4: **A VISIT WITH MRS. SLASKI** 41

CHAPTER 5: **LOGAN'S LITTLE HELPER** 59

CHAPTER 6: **THE MAGIC LANTERN** 69

CHAPTER 7: **SUPPER WITH THE BRUNAS** 85

CHAPTER 8: **THE GHOST RETURNS** 97

CHAPTER 9: **LOST AND FOUND** 111

◦ A FLASH OF WHITE ◦

Logan Pryce knelt down on the bank of Juniper Creek and sifted through the carpet of stones. Big ones, little ones, bumpy ones, flat ones—there were so many to choose from!

"Logan, it's still your turn," his sister Tess reminded him. She hoisted up the hem of her flower-print dress as she waded barefoot through the cool water.

"My stone went four skips, and Tess's stone went five," Anthony Bruna said, who was Logan's best friend.

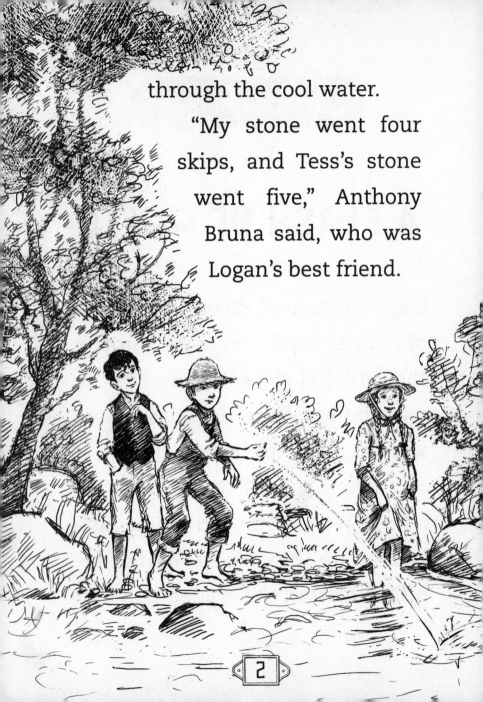

"Then mine shall go six skips!" Logan announced.

He picked up a smooth gray stone the size of a silver dollar and pitched it into the creek. *Splish! Splash! Splosh!* It sank below the surface after three skips.

"Aw, that's too bad," Anthony said, patting Logan on the back. "Do you want to try again?"

"Nah. Let's fish instead," Logan suggested.

"I could run home and get us a couple of poles?" Anthony offered.

Tess frowned at the sky, which swirled with gold and purple clouds.

"The sun's starting to go down. Pa will be home soon for supper. Your pa, too, Anthony."

"I guess we'd better head on home, then," said Logan, peering around for his dog. "Wait, where's Skeeter?"

"He's probably chasing rabbits," replied Tess. She cupped her hands over her mouth. "Skeeter!"

"*Skeeter!*" Logan shouted.

"*Skeeter!*" Anthony joined in.

Woof! Woof! Woof! They heard Skeeter's bark coming from the forest next to the creek.

"Skeeter! Come on, boy!" Logan called out as loudly as he could.

Woof! Skeeter barked again. But still, he didn't appear.

Logan sighed and marched into the forest to look for him. Tess and Anthony followed. Beech and sugar maple trees made a canopy over their heads and blocked out the sun. Deep shadows stretched across the dirt path and made it seem like night.

Logan wished he had a lamp to

light the way. "Skeeter! Time to go home!"

Just then Skeeter burst out of a thicket of witch hazel shrubs. Burrs

and leaves clung to his honey-colored coat.

"There you are, boy! Where have you been?" Logan asked.

Skeeter barked, spun around, and ran back into the shrubs.

"Skeeter! Wait!" Logan ordered.

"Maybe he found something," said Tess.

"Maybe it's treasure!" Anthony added.

The three
children dashed
after Skeeter. They
came upon him
sitting at the base
of a maple tree,
his tail whipping
back and forth.

"What is it, boy?"
asked Logan.

Skeeter pointed his nose to the
sky. Logan followed his gaze.

A flash of white rippled through
the highest branches of the tree.
The leaves shook and shivered.

Then everything was silent and still.

"D-did you both see that?" Logan stammered.

Tess crossed her arms over her chest and stepped back to get a better look. "What was it?"

"I think it was a ghost!" Anthony exclaimed.

◦ BOO! ◦

"Logan! Tess! You're late!" Ma said as soon as they walked through the door. She, Pa, Drew, and Annie sat around the kitchen table helping themselves to beans, biscuits, and corn on the cob.

"Logan and Tess are in trouble; Logan and Tess are in trouble," chanted Drew, who was eleven.

"Lolo and Tessie are *not* in trouble!" Annie cried out. At four, she was the youngest member of the Pryce family. Logan, who was eight, and Tess, who was nine, were right in the middle.

"No one's in trouble. Let's all sit

down so we can enjoy the fine meal Ma made for us," said Pa. Soda ash and limestone covered his overalls, and tired lines furrowed his brow. He worked at a glass factory in Sherman, which was a couple of hours away by horse and buggy.

Logan and Tess hung their straw hats on hooks and joined everyone at the table. They had already washed their hands at the pump outside. Skeeter hunkered down next to Logan's chair and sniffed at the floor, searching for food.

"So where were you two, anyway?" Ma asked as she lit the kerosene lamp.

"We went over to Juniper Creek

with Anthony," Logan replied. He tore off a piece of biscuit and dangled it under the table. Skeeter gobbled it up immediately.

Annie's face lit up. "Did you see any turtles? Or minnows? Or other critters?"

Logan snuck a quick glance at Tess. "Well, we *did* see something strange."

"*Shhh,*" Tess said, elbowing him.

"What was it?" asked Drew.

"A ghost!" Logan blurted out.

Annie clutched her cloth doll. "Ghosts are just pretend. Aren't they, Mrs. Wigglesworth?" she said.

"Annie's right. There's no such things as ghosts," declared Ma.

"I read a ghost story the other day, and the ghost turned out to be a real person," said Tess.

"I don't know. Folks around here have mentioned seeing the ghost of Juniper Creek," Drew piped up. "They say it's been around for a hundred years and that it's mighty scary. Was it scary, Logan?"

"No!" Logan practically yelled. Skeeter barked.

"Drew, you are frightening everyone. Why don't we talk about something else? Dale, how was your day at work?" Ma asked, turning to Pa.

"It was good," replied Pa. "Mr. Garrison still has me in

charge of loading up the
furnace with sand and
limestone and so forth.

But we talked about how I might be a glassblower someday."

Ma smiled. "How wonderful!"

"You'll be running the place soon, Pa!" Tess said proudly.

Drew bent his head to Logan's. "Guess what?" he whispered.

"What?" Logan whispered back.

"*Boo!*" Drew shouted, raising his arms in the air. He roared with laughter.

"*Andrew Henry Pryce!*" Pa chided him.

Logan scowled at Drew and bit into his corn on the cob.

Surely, Drew was lying. There was no such thing as the ghost of Juniper Creek.

Was there?

CHAPTER 3

• THE GHOST TRAP •

That night, Logan had a very scary dream. In the dream, he and Anthony were fishing in Juniper Creek when an odd noise startled them. They turned around and saw a white figure floating toward them from the forest. It was a ghost! The boys screamed and ran. The ghost chased after them, crying, "*Boo!*"

Logan woke up with a start and glanced wildly around the room. There were no ghosts, just Drew snoring in his bed. The first light of dawn slanted through the windows. A rooster crowed in the distance.

Wide awake, Logan got dressed and tiptoed down the stairs. As he hurried outside, Skeeter rose from his usual spot in front of the cast-iron stove and followed with a quiet pattering of paws. They crossed the yard and headed for the barn.

Inside the barn, the horses, Lightning and Buttercup, pricked their ears and made soft nickering sounds. The cows, Daisy Mae and Miss Moo, bobbed their heads. The animals were used to seeing Logan

at this early hour, since it was when he did his morning chores.

"I'll help you in a minute, ladies and gentlemen. I mean, gentle*man*," Logan corrected himself. Skeeter was the only boy of the bunch.

Logan went over to his Fix-It Shop and settled in. The shop took up a stall in the corner of the barn.

It was where he mended old things and invented new things.

His scary dream had given him an idea. He would invent a trap to catch the ghost of Juniper Creek. He wasn't sure the ghost really existed. Maybe Drew had made up the whole thing. But it couldn't hurt to build it, just in case.

Logan sifted
through a crate of
random objects. A
broken pinwheel.
An empty inkwell.
Barrel staves.
A piece of rope. Doorknobs.
A pencil box.

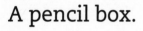

A *pencil box might be just the thing*, he thought.

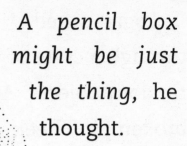

He picked it up and placed it on his worktable to study it. He measured it with his folding rule. Was it big enough to trap a ghost? How would he lure the ghost into it? And once the ghost was inside, how would he keep the lid closed?

He plucked several barrel staves out of the crate and built a teepee. The wooden strips were sturdy and could come in handy, maybe to rig the trap?

Buttercup gave a sudden snort. Logan glanced up, startled. His teepee

collapsed, and the barrel staves tumbled to the ground.

"What's wrong, girl?" he called out to the mare.

Buttercup's eyes were fixed intently on something on the

ceiling. She stamped her feet and flared her nostrils. Lightning did the same. Skeeter barked.

Goose bumps prickled on Logan's arms as he slowly looked up.

There was nothing there—not even a bird or a mouse.

The barn doors creaked open. Logan gave a surprised yell.

"Logan, it's just me!" Tess said, rushing up to him. She wore her

school clothes, and her brown hair hung in neat braids. "What's wrong? Why did you scream?"

"N-no reason. What are you doing here?" Logan asked in a shaky voice.

"I finished up my chores, so I thought I'd help you with yours," Tess replied.

"Oh. Thanks."

They got busy brushing the horses. As they worked, Logan wondered: What had spooked the animals so? Was it the ghost?

CHAPTER 4

A VISIT WITH MRS. SLASKI

On their way to school, Logan and Tess had to stop by their neighbor Mrs. Slaski's house. Drew went on ahead because it was his turn to bring in a pail of milk for the class to share. The school was a mile away, and the walk took a good twenty minutes on dirt roads. Logan could hear the milk slosh back and forth as Drew left.

Mrs. Slaski's house was tucked away on a hill. Her garden was a rainbow of zinnias, black-eyed Susans, and other late-summer flowers. Butterflies flitted around.

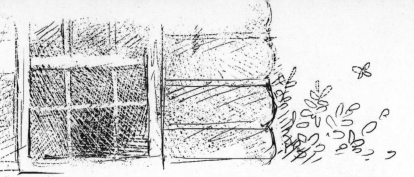

"So why, again, do we need to see Mrs. Slaski?" Logan asked Tess as they knocked on her door.

Tess held up a parcel wrapped in brown paper. "Because Ma wants us to drop off this package. It's a dress she mended for Mrs. Slaski."

"Oh!"

Just recently, Ma had started doing some sewing for extra money. After Pa stopped farming their land, he and Ma had to take on small jobs

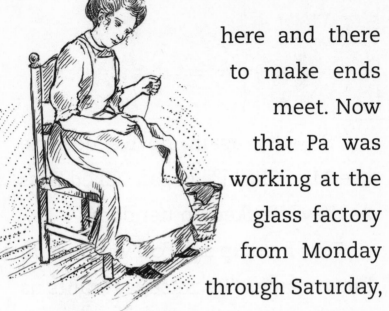

here and there to make ends meet. Now that Pa was working at the glass factory from Monday through Saturday, things were getting gradually better.

Last week, Ma had even bought new socks for the whole family at the general store.

The Pryces weren't the only ones to give up on their farms. Many farmers in Maple Ridge had let their fields go fallow so they could work in a big-city factory like Pa. It was the only way for them to make enough money to provide for their families.

Logan and Tess heard footsteps inside the house. The door opened, and then Mrs. Slaski smiled down at them.

"Why, hello there, children! Your mother told me you'd be dropping by. Come in! Come in!" she said, wiping her hands on her apron.

"We have to be at school by eight o'clock sharp," said Tess.

"Well, that's just enough time for you both to have a slice of gingerbread. Today is my baking day."

"Thanks!" Logan couldn't resist gingerbread.

"Yes, thank you," Tess added politely.

Inside, Mrs. Slaski brought them

thick pieces of warm gingerbread
on dainty china plates. Logan
and Tess set their lunch pails and
schoolbooks on the floor and dug in
eagerly.

Mrs. Slaski unwrapped the parcel and held up a pretty blue dress. "Your mother did fine work! The new hem is as straight as a pin."

"Ma's been teaching me how to sew," Tess told her.

"My mother taught me how to sew too. Of course, that was a very long time ago, and my eyes aren't what they used to be," Mrs. Slaski said.

A *very long time ago*. Logan recalled Drew saying that the ghost of Juniper Creek had been around for a hundred years. Logan counted on his fingers and guessed that Mrs. Slaski was probably that old too. She might know something.

"Mrs. Slaski? Did you ever hear about . . . when you were little, do

you remember seeing a . . ." Logan
took a deep breath. *"Ghost?"*

Tess coughed.

"You mean the ghost of Juniper
Creek?" said Mrs. Slaski. "My friend

Trudy and I used to play at the creek when we were girls. We saw something there, once. She said it was the ghost. But I think it was just an optical illusion."

"An optical *what?*" Logan asked, confused.

"An optical illusion is when you *think* you see something, but it's just your eyes playing tricks on you," Tess explained smartly.

Soon, it was time to leave for school. "Is Snowball here? Can I pet her?" Logan asked, remembering Mrs. Slaski's pet cat.

Mrs. Slaski sighed. "Snowball ran away."

"Oh no!" Tess cried out.

"She's been gone since last Tuesday. I fear she's never coming back," Mrs. Slaski said, dabbing her eyes with a handkerchief.

Logan thought about the time when Skeeter ran away for a whole day. Logan had holed up in his Fix-It Shop and put together a dog trap out of a coffee crate and a couple of beef bones. He had found Skeeter that night, sniffing around the crate.

Maybe he could build a trap for Snowball, too? Now all he had to do was build two traps: a cat trap and a ghost trap!

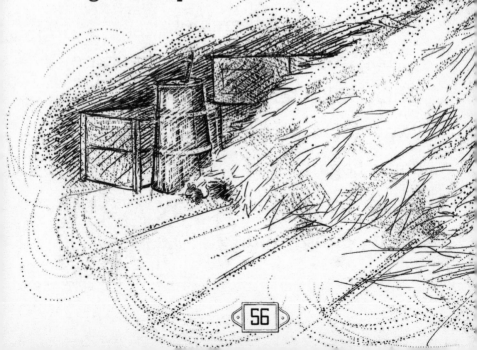

CHAPTER 5

LOGAN'S LITTLE HELPER

After school, Logan hunkered down on an old tree stump just outside the barn. In front of him were different objects for making his two traps.

He had found a fruit crate to use for the cat trap. He had also found a couple of blue jay feathers to put inside it, since cats liked birds. The

feathers might attract Snowball and lure her inside the trap.

For the ghost trap, Logan had decided that the pencil box was too small and instead chose an old toy chest. The problem was what to put inside it. If feathers attracted cats,

what attracted ghosts? A candle?
A phonograph that played spooky
music? He really didn't know much
about ghosts.

"What are you doing,
Lolo?" Annie skipped
toward him with
a pail full of
wildflowers.

She wore a hand-me-down dress from Tess that was several sizes too big for her. A wreath of daisies circled her head.

"Projects," Logan replied with a shrug.

"But why aren't you in your Fix-It Shop, like always?" asked Annie.

"Um . . ." Logan didn't want to admit that he was too scared to be alone in the barn. *Something* had frightened the animals earlier. "I felt like making my projects outside," he fibbed.

"What are you making?"

Logan patted the fruit crate. "Well, this is going to be a trap for Mrs. Slaski's cat, Snowball. She ran away. I'm putting things inside it that cats like. Bird feathers, maybe a tin of sardines." He wasn't so

sure about the sardines. Ma wasn't likely to give up an expensive food item just to catch a cat.

"What about catnip?" Annie suggested.

"Catnip?"

Annie set her pail on the ground and skipped toward the henhouse. She returned a moment later with a fistful of green leaves.

"Pa said it grows wild all over our farm. Kitties love it!" she explained.

Logan took the leaves from

her and stuffed them in the crate.
"Thanks!"

Annie pointed to the toy chest.
"Is that a kitty trap too?"

Logan was about to explain that
the chest was going to be a ghost

trap. But he didn't want to frighten his little sister. "Nah. I'm not sure what I'll do with it yet."

"Maybe you could make a bed for Mrs. Wigglesworth!"

"Maybe."

Logan continued working. Annie plopped down on the tree trunk next to him and watched in silence.

After a while, Skeeter wandered over and lay down in a warm patch of sunlight. Annie wove a wreath of wildflowers and perched it on his head. The sight made Logan laugh so hard that he almost forgot about the ghost of Juniper Creek and Mrs. Slaski's missing cat.

CHAPTER 6

THE
MAGIC LANTERN

On Saturday morning, Logan and Drew walked over to Mayberry's General Store on Main Street. Logan carried a dozen jars of Ma's home-made jam. The jars clinked against one another in the basket, and Logan reminded himself not to drop them. Drew carried a crock of butter that Tess had churned before breakfast.

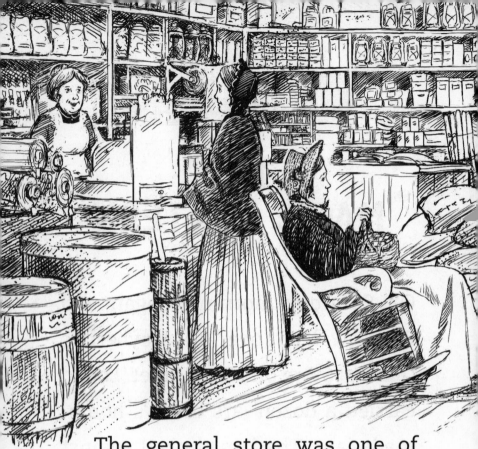

The general store was one of
Logan's favorite places in Maple
Ridge. There, Mr. and Mrs. Mayberry
sold groceries, clothing, books, tools,
and just about everything else. It

also served as a post office and had
the only telephone in town. People
liked to sit in the rocking chairs and
catch up on events.

Mrs. Mayberry stood behind the counter measuring a length of silk ribbon. She waved when she saw the boys. "Why, hello there! Did your ma send you over with some things to trade?" she asked cheerfully.

"Butter and jam. There are two kinds of jam, peach and blueberry. Ma asked if she could have some salt, maple

syrup, lamp oil, and vinegar, in exchange," Drew rattled off.

"Coming right up. I just

have to get the kerosene in the back room," Mrs. Mayberry replied.

She bustled away.

While they waited, Drew played with a toy cannon. Logan admired the jars of colorful penny candies.

There was a strange object next to the candies. It was a big brass box with tubes and knobs sticking out of it. A handwritten sign read: $5.

What could it be? wondered Logan.

Mrs. Mayberry returned with a can of kerosene. "Here's your lamp oil. Oh, I see you've discovered the magic lantern," she said to Logan.

Logan quickly perked up. "Magic lantern?"

Mrs. Mayberry nodded. "This one belonged to a magician named Alonzo the Great. He used it for his ghost shows."

"What are ghost shows?" asked Drew.

"They have them in big city theaters and dime museums. Magicians like Alonzo the Great use

the magic lanterns to create optical illusions of ghosts," Mrs. Mayberry explained.

Optical illusions. Logan remembered that an optical illusion was

when you *thought* you saw something, but it was just your eyes playing a trick on you.

"So they're not real? The ghosts in these ghost shows?" said Logan.

Mrs. Mayberry chuckled and shook her head. "No, not at all."

Logan touched the magic lantern

and wondered how it worked. It was the exact opposite of his ghost trap. It made ghosts appear instead of disappear!

"Logan's a big fraidy-cat about ghosts," Drew told Mrs. Mayberry with a wink.

"*I am not!*" protested Logan.

"In fact, he saw a ghost at the creek the other day. He wouldn't stop yammering about it!" Drew teased.

"The ghost of Juniper Creek? I remember my mother mentioning it when I was little," Mrs. Mayberry said.

Logan blinked. "You mean . . . your ma *saw* it?"

"No, but she knew other folks who did," Mrs. Mayberry replied with a faraway look. She smiled and shook her head. "Enough about ghosts! Let me get those other items for your ma. I'll throw in some penny candies for you boys and your sisters, too!"

"Thanks, Mrs. Mayberry!" Dale grinned.

Logan nodded his thanks. But his mind was racing with thoughts

about the ghost of Juniper Creek. It no longer seemed like one of Drew's tall tales. Other people had seen it.

Logan needed to finish his ghost trap as soon as possible!

CHAPTER 7

SUPPER WITH THE BRUNAS

That night, the entire Pryce family was invited to the Brunas' house for supper.

There were ten of them in all: Pa, Ma, Drew, Tess, Logan, Annie, Mr. Bruna, Mrs. Bruna, Anthony, and Anthony's little sister, Isabella, who was Annie's age. They crowded around several small tables that had

been pushed together and covered
with lace cloth.

Mrs. Bruna passed around large

platters. "Please, eat! *Mangia!* I made peas and eggs, fried fish, and vegetables from the garden."

"This all looks delicious, Elena. It was very kind of you to cook for us," said Ma.

Everyone began eating. Ma asked Mrs. Bruna about the food she and Mr. Bruna had grown up with in Italy. Tess and Drew had a contest to see who could come up with the longest word. Annie and Isabella made up adventures for their dolls. Pa and Mr. Bruna joked about something they had seen that morning in Sherman. Mr. Bruna worked at the steel mill,

which was near Pa's glass factory, and they often rode to and from work together.

Logan scooted his chair closer to Anthony's. "I have a mission for us for later," he whispered.

"What kind of mission?" Anthony asked curiously.

"I built a special trap so we can catch the ghost of Juniper Creek,"

replied Logan. "I brought it with me. It's in that gunnysack over there. We need to go over to the creek and set it up."

"Gosh, that sounds dangerous!"

"It might be. But we have to be brave. Are you with me?"

Anthony gulped and nodded. "I am with you."

"What are you little kids talking about?" Drew asked, leaning over.

"*Little kids?*" gasped Logan.

"We are about to do something very brave and dangerous," Anthony said huffily.

Drew raised his eyebrows. "Oh? What are you up to?"

Logan told Drew about the mission. When he was finished, Drew whistled.

"That *does* sound dangerous. But if you succeed, you'll be heroes in this town!"

Heroes? Logan sat up very straight. He liked the sound of that!

CHAPTER 8

THE GHOST RETURNS

After supper, Logan and Anthony got permission from their parents to play outside.

"Stay close to the house and take one of the lamps with you. It's getting dark!" Mrs. Bruna called after them.

"Yes, Mama," Anthony promised.

The boys hurried out the back

door and made their way toward
Juniper Creek. The creek ran along
the south side of the Brunas'
property, and the forest was just
beyond. Anthony had brought along
a kerosene lamp. Logan clutched

the gunnysack that held his ghost trap. He had finished working on it that afternoon.

Logan had set aside his *other* trap, which was the trap for catching Mrs. Slaski's missing cat. He would finish it tomorrow and put it somewhere in her yard. He had even saved a piece of fish from tonight's meal to place inside the trap. It was in the pocket of his dungarees, wrapped in a handkerchief.

The moon shone down and helped to light their way as they neared the creek. The air was cool and smelled like firewood and apples. Crickets hummed. Bullfrogs twanged.

Somewhere, a coyote howled. It was a long, shrill sound and made Logan shudder. "Maybe we should

go back," he said nervously.

"But you said we had to be brave," Anthony reminded him.

"I guess so. All right. Let us march on!" Logan lifted his gunnysack like a flag.

They soon reached the creek. They walked along the bank until they were at the edge of the forest.

It was pitch black in the stand of beech and sugar maples. Anthony stopped and swung his lamp in a wide arc. Logan squinted. He could

see spidery shrubs and branches like spindly arms—but nothing else.

"Where do you want to set up the trap?" Anthony asked.

"Maybe under that tree," Logan replied, pointing. "I think we're close to the spot where we saw the . . . *you know.*"

He and Anthony got busy. Logan placed the ghost trap on the mossy ground and propped open the lid. Inside was a sprig of catnip that Annie must have put there earlier. If catnip could lure cats, then maybe it could lure ghosts, too? It was a

crazy thought, but he had run out
of ideas—and time.

Two long pieces of string came
from the lid. "You take one piece,
and I'll take the other," Logan told
Anthony. "As soon as the ghost is in
the trap, we pull! That will slam the
lid shut."

"O-okay."

Holding on to their strings, the boys hid behind some shrubs and waited. And waited. And waited.

"Maybe you were right. Maybe we should go back," Anthony whispered.

Logan frowned. "Wait! I think I hear something."

A sudden breeze shook the leaves on the trees. The flame of the lamp flickered.

A cloud passed across the moon. From high up in the branches, two golden eyes blinked down at Logan and Anthony.

It was the ghost!

CHAPTER 9

•LOST AND FOUND•

Anthony jabbed Logan with his elbow. "Logan! *Pssst!* Is that . . . ?"

"I—I think so!" said Logan, terrified.

A moan rose in the air. The boys shrieked and jumped to their feet.

A figure leapt out at them from behind the tree, laughing. It wasn't a ghost at all. It was Drew!

"*That is not funny!*" Logan said hotly.

"Not funny at all!" Anthony agreed.

Drew doubled over with laughter. "Relax! There's no such thing as the ghost of Juniper Creek. That's just a story that was made up by a bunch of fraidy-cats!"

Just then something *else* rustled in the darkness.

Drew stopped laughing. "What... was... *that?*" he whispered.

The shrubs stirred and parted,

revealing a flash of white. It was the same flash of white that Logan and Anthony had seen the other day.

Drew screamed and took off running.

The flash of white stepped out of
the shrubs. Its golden eyes shone in
the moonlight.

It opened its mouth . . . and
meowed.

"Snowball!" Logan cried out, relieved.

Mrs. Slaski's cat pranced over to Logan and pawed at his dungarees. After a moment, he realized that she could smell the piece of fish in his pocket.

Chuckling, Logan pulled it out and gave it to Snowball. She gobbled it up.

"Gosh. We were scared of a cat?" said Anthony, shaking his head.

Snowball sniffed at the ghost

trap. She stuck in her paw and teased out the piece of catnip.

Logan couldn't believe his eyes. *Snowball* was the ghost of Juniper Creek. He wouldn't need to finish his cat trap after all.

"She's been missing since last Tuesday. Mrs. Slaski will be mighty glad to see her," he told Anthony.

"That's for sure. Say, where's your brother?" Anthony said, peering around.

"I think he went back to your house. *He* turned out to be the fraidiest-cat of all!"

The two boys grinned at each other as they picked up Snowball and the ghost trap and started for home.

Check out the next

TALES FROM MAPLE RIDGE

adventure!

HERE'S A SNEAK PEEK!

Logan Pryce paused on the wooded path and picked up a spindly branch.

Logan's brother, Drew, turned around. "What do you need a stick for, anyway?"

"It's for my new fix-it project," replied Logan.

"What are you fixing up?"

"It's a highly guarded secret. All shall be revealed soon!"

Drew rolled his eyes. Being a big brother, he rolled his eyes a lot.

Logan's new fix-it project was a sled! But he didn't want Drew to know, because it was going to be a surprise for the whole family. Logan had found the broken old sled in the barn, and he had been tinkering with it in his Fix-It Shop. He needed some parts, like a few sturdy branches and a length of strong rope.

They continued down the path. A chill had settled in the air. Logan could feel it even through his wool cap, peacoat, and knickers.

Drew paused in front of a huge fallen tree. "This is a rock elm. These make for mighty good firewood. I wish I'd brought an ax," said Drew. Keeping the wood box full was one of his regular chores.

Logan glanced over his shoulder. Behind them on the path, he could see the sun setting in the sky. "We should go," he told Drew.

Drew crouched down to inspect the fallen tree. "What are you afraid of, Logan? Getting lost in the dark, scary forest?" he joked.